Great Expectations

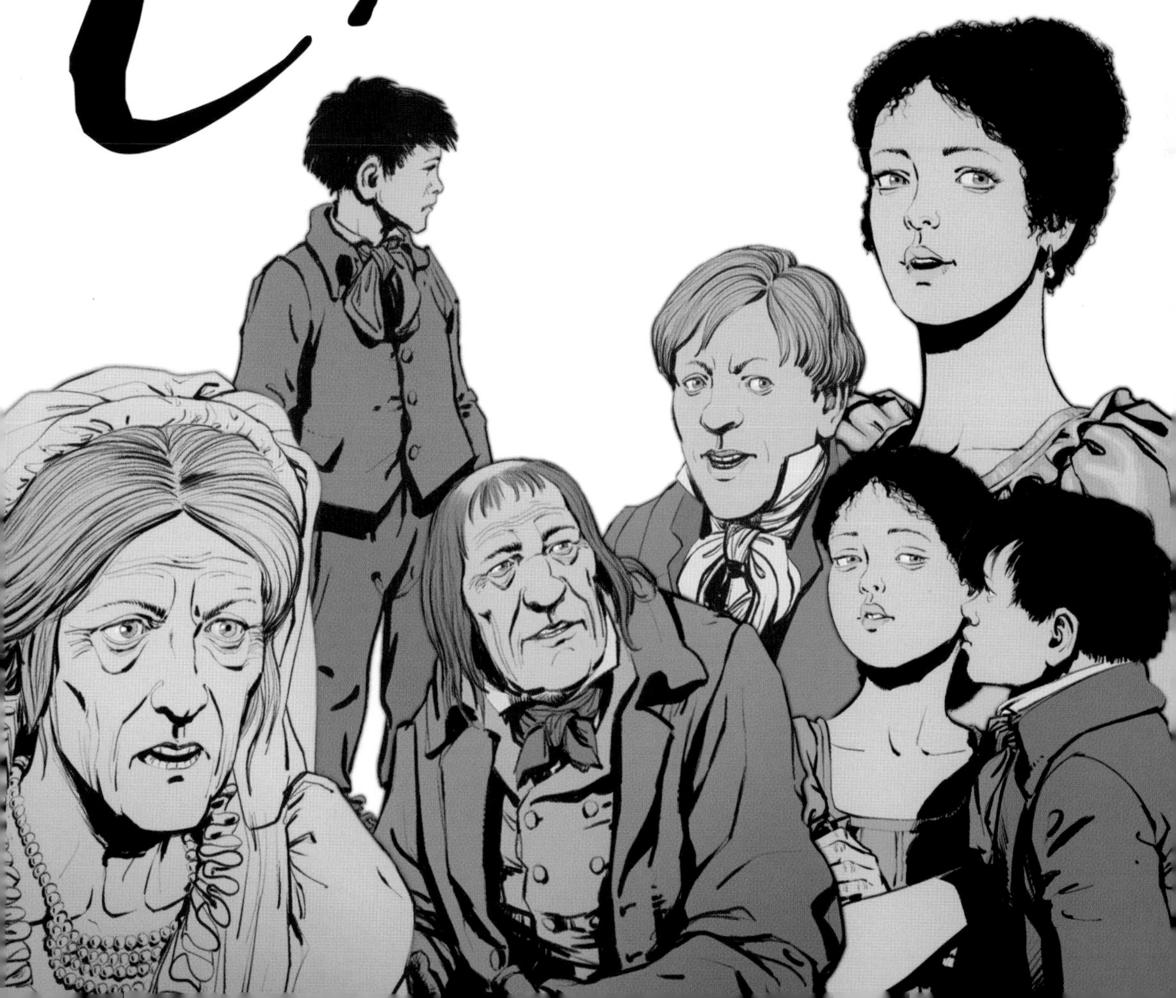

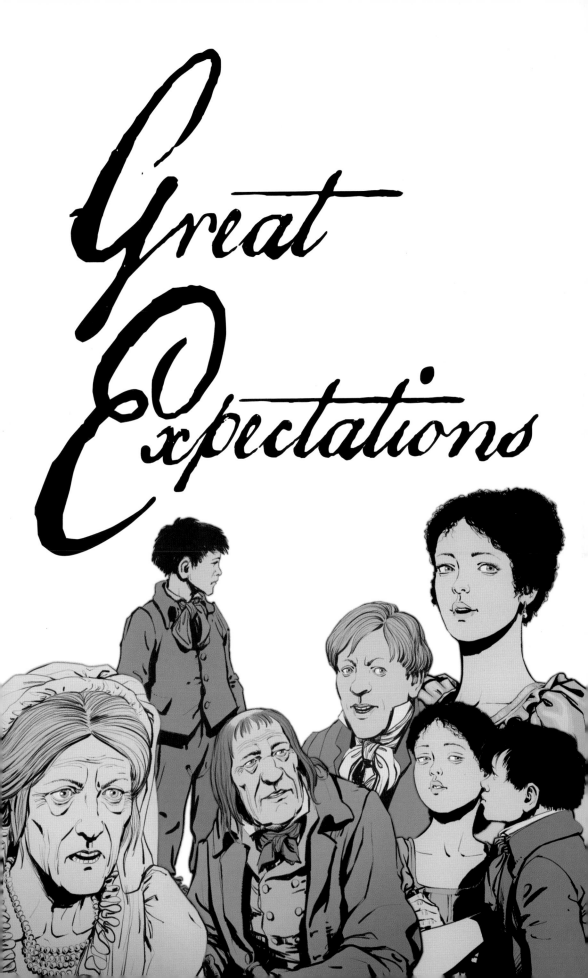

Artists: Penko Gelev

Sotir Gelev

First edition for North America (including Canada and Mexico),
Philippine Islands, and Puerto Rico published in 2011
by Barron's Educational Series, Inc.

All inquiries should be addressed to:
Barron's Educational Series, Inc.
250 Wireless Blvd.
Hauppauge, NY 11788
www.barronseduc.com

ISBN (Hardcover): 978-0-7641-6304-3
ISBN (Paperback): 978-0-7641-4452-3

Library of Congress Control No.: 2011920871

Picture credits:
p. 40 © Coll. Jaime Abecasis/Topfoto.co.uk
p. 43 © 2000 Topham Picturepoint/TopFoto.co.uk
p. 45 Carolyn Franklin

Every effort has been made to trace copyright holders. The Salariya Book Company apologizes for any
omissions and would be pleased, in such cases, to add an acknowledgement in future editions.

Date of Manufacture: July 2011
Manufactured by: Leo Paper Products, Ltd., Heshan, Guangdong, China

Printed and bound in China
9 8 7 6 5 4 3 2 1

Great Expectations

Charles Dickens

Illustrated by

Penko Gelev

BARRON'S

Retold by

Jacqueline Morley

Series created and designed by

David Salariya

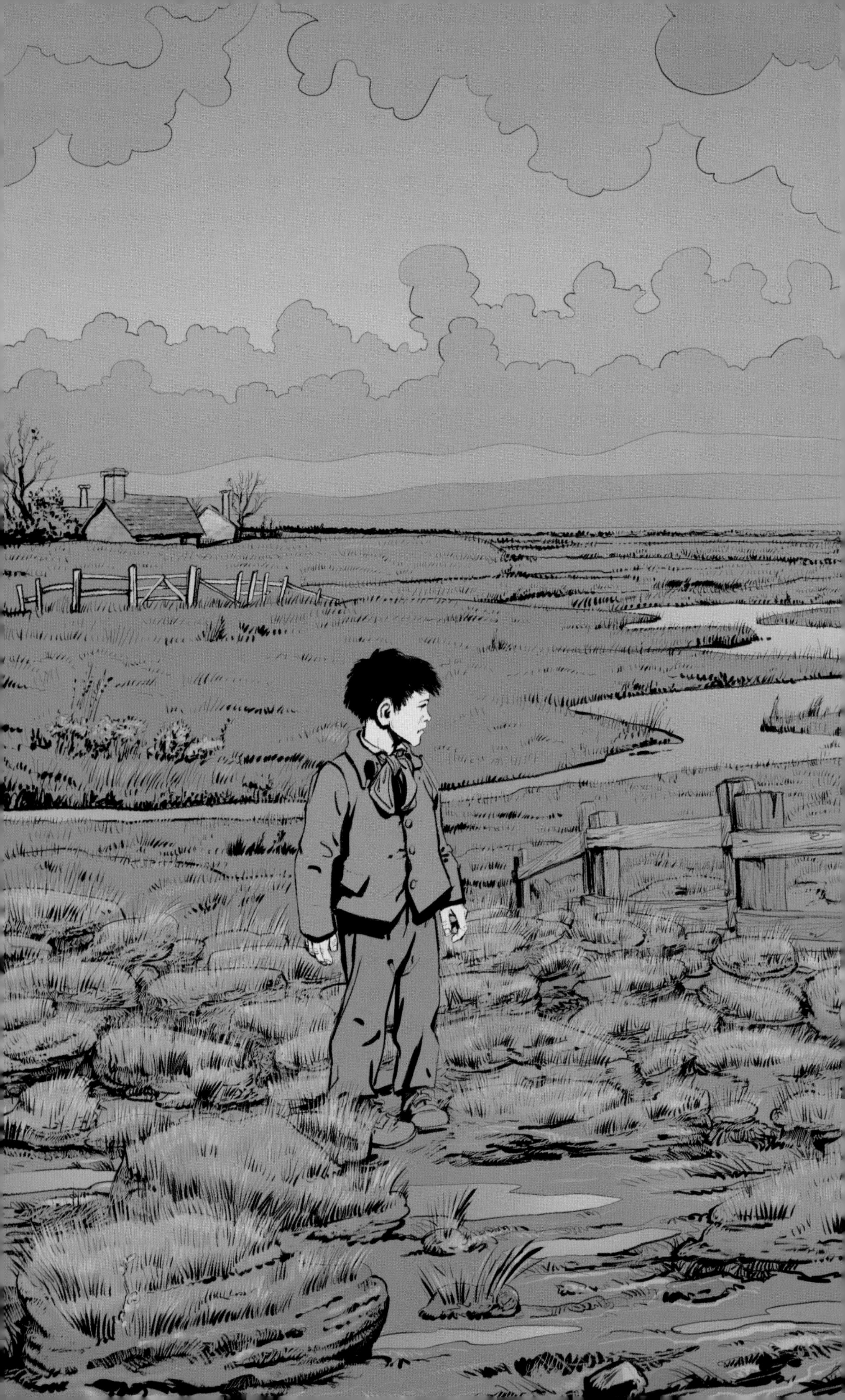

Ours was the marsh country, down by the river, within twenty miles of the sea. The dark flat wilderness beyond the churchyard was the marshes. The low leaden line beyond was the river. The distant savage lair from which the wind was rushing was the sea. And the small bundle of shivers growing afraid of it all and beginning to cry was Pip.

CHARACTERS

Mrs. Joe Gargery, Pip's sister

Pip as a child

Pip as a young man

Joe Gargery, blacksmith, Pip's brother-in-law

Abel Magwitch, a convict

Compeyson, Magwitch's enemy

Mr. Pumblechook, Joe's uncle

Miss Havisham, an elderly spinster

Estella, her adopted daughter

Biddy, a village girl

Mr. Jaggers, a London lawyer

Molly, Mr. Jaggers's housekeeper

Mr. Wemmick, Jaggers's clerk

Herbert Pocket, a relative of Miss Havisham

Bentley Drummle, a wealthy young man

THE CHURCHYARD

One chilly Christmas Eve, a small boy stood among the tombstones in a lonely churchyard.

It was a bleak, windswept place overlooking the Kentish[1] marshes that stretched away, flat and sad, towards the River Thames.[2]

I was that small boy—named Philip Pirrip after my father, but always known as Pip. That afternoon was to shape the rest of my life.

PHILIP PIRRIP
Late of this Parish
Also Georgiana
Wife of the Above

My parents died when I was very young, so I had no memory of them. My idea of what they were like—square and stiff or thin and curly—was taken from the lettering on their grave.

The sky was darkening and the wind rose. The loneliness of the place grew suddenly so frightening that I began to cry.

Just then...

Hold your noise! Keep still, you little devil, or I'll cut your throat!

Oh! Don't cut my throat, sir. Pray don't do it, sir.

1. Kentish: in the county of Kent, in the southeast corner of England (see map on page 45).
2. Thames: the major river that flows through London and reaches the sea between the counties of Kent and Essex.

THE CONVICT

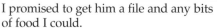

1. wittles: victuals (food). The convict has a Cockney (working-class London) accent.

If it warn't for me you'd have been in the churchyard long ago.[1] Who brought you up by hand?

You did.

I'd never do it again! It's bad enough to be a blacksmith's wife without being your mother.

Joe and I were eating our supper together when we heard gunfire.

CRACK!

What does that mean, Joe?

There was a convict off[2] last night. And now, it appears, they're firing warning of another.

It's from the Hulks.[3]

People are put in the Hulks because they murder and rob and forge and do all sorts of bad.

I did not sleep for terror of the young man who might tear me open. At dawn I crept downstairs to the pantry.

A pork pie! Perhaps it won't be missed.

It's not him. It must be the terrible young man!

My convict fell on the food like a hungry dog.

Won't you leave any for the young man? He looked very hungry.

I thought it was you at first. He's dressed like you. He had a badly bruised face.

Not here?

I've no young man. Who did you see?

Yes, there!

It's Compeyson! Show me the way he went. I'll pull him down like a bloodhound!

He began filing his leg-iron like a madman, not minding how he cut into his leg. I fled.

---

1. you'd have been in the churchyard long ago: you'd have been dead and buried.
2. a convict off: a convict escaped.
3. Hulks: ships no longer seaworthy that were moored on the Thames and Medway rivers to serve as prisons (see page 47).

RECAPTURED

Joe's Uncle Pumblechook, who was always invited for Christmas, lectured me as usual, and made the Christmas meal a misery for me.

> Be grateful, boy, to them which brought you up by hand.

> Why is it that the young are never grateful?

> You must taste a delicious present of Uncle Pumblechook's—a savory pork pie.

My crime was about to be discovered! I made a dash for the door…

…and ran straight into a row of soldiers on the doorstep.

> Excuse me, ladies and gentlemen. I want the blacksmith.

They were hunting two escaped convicts, and needed Joe to mend their handcuffs. The pork pie was quite forgotten as everyone followed Joe into the forge.[1]

> How far might you call yourselves[2] from the marshes?

> Just a mile.

Joe suggested that he and I should go down with the soldiers and see how the hunt went.

> If you bring that boy back with his head blown to bits by a musket,[3] don't look to me to put it together.

> That's not so bad. We'll close in on 'em about dusk.

> Suppose my convict thinks it's me that's led the soldiers here?

We went up and down banks, splashed across dykes[4] and over the open marshes.

---

1. forge: a blacksmith's workshop. 2. How far might you call yourselves?: How far do you think you are?
3. musket: a long-barrelled handgun. 4: dykes: walls made of earth to keep the seawater off the land.

We heard shouts from a distance. There seemed to be two voices.

The soldiers lit torches. In the sudden light my convict saw me and looked at me hard.

As the convicts were rowed back to the Hulk, mine turned his head and looked at me still.

1. mind: remember, take notice. Pip's convict has captured his enemy, intending to hand him over to the soldiers. He is determined that Compeyson must not get away, even though he himself will be captured at the same time.
2. It may…suspicion: He doesn't want Pip to be blamed for stealing the food.

A Strange Invitation

Three years later…

Now if this boy an't grateful this night, he never will be!

Miss Havisham wants this boy to go and play at her house.

And he had better play there, or I'll work[1] him.

Miss Havisham was an immensely rich and grim lady who never left her house.

Miss Havisham? I wonder how she came to know Pip?

Noodle![2] Who said she knew him?

Isn't it just possible, seeing as Uncle Pumblechook is her tenant,[3] she might ask him if he knew of a boy to go and play there?

And Uncle Pumblechook, thinking this boy's fortune may be made by Miss Havisham, has offered to take him there.

Lor-a-mussy me![4] Grimed with crock[5] and dirt from the hair of his head to the sole of his foot!

Why on earth am I going to play at Miss Havisham's?

Trussed up tight in my best suit, I was bundled into Uncle Pumblechook's chaise-cart.[6]

1. work: beat.
2. noodle: a foolish person
3. tenant: a person who rents a house or land owned by another person.
4. Lor-a-mussy me!: Lord have mercy on me.
5. crock: soot.   6. chaise-cart: light two-wheeled carriage.

Uncle Pumblechook pulled the doorbell as I peered through the gates.

A young lady came towards us with a key.

This is Pip.

Come in, Pip.

Oh! Did *you* wish to see Miss Havisham?

If Miss Havisham wished to see me.

Ah, but you see she don't.

Don't loiter, boy.

How grand she is, calling me "boy" as if she were years older than me.

I followed this haughty person into the house, which was all in the dark.

Go in.

After you, miss.

Don't be ridiculous, boy; I am not going in.

Who is it?

Pip, ma'am.

She left me in the dark. I knocked and went in. The room was candle-lit; there was no chink of daylight. The strangest-looking lady was seated at a dressing table.

13

Miss Havisham

She wore a wedding dress, yellowed with age, and she was old and withered too.

I saw that her watch had stopped at twenty to nine. The clock had stopped at the same time.

1. sullen and obstinate: sulky and stubborn.
2. laboring: working-class.

Well? You can break his heart.

He calls the knaves Jacks,[1] this boy. And what coarse[2] hands he has. And what thick boots!

You say nothing of her. What do you think of her?

I don't like to say.

Tell me in my ear.

I think she is very proud.

Anything else?

I think she is very insulting.

Anything else?

I think she is very pretty.

Anything else?

I think I should like to go home.

Estella brought me something to eat in the yard, as if I were a dog. While she was gone I hid my face and sobbed.

Why don't you cry?

Because I don't want to.

You do. You have been crying till you are half blind, and you are near crying now.

I went home feeling I was coarse and common and that everything about me—my home, the forge and even dear Joe—was common, too.

1. knaves and Jacks: Jacks is a lower form of the term knaves in cardplaying.
2. coarse: rough.

THE WEDDING FEAST

Next week by appointment I returned to Miss Havisham's.

Well? Am I pretty?

Yes.

Am I insulting?

Not so much as you were the last time.

No?

SLAP!

Why don't you cry again, you little wretch?

Because I'll never cry for you again.

I lied. I was inwardly crying for her then, and in the future she was to cost me much more pain.

How do *you* come here?

Miss Havisham sent for me, sir.

Well! Behave yourself. I have a pretty large experience of boys.

Miss Havisham and her room were just as I had left them.

Since you are unwilling to play, are you willing to work?

Yes, ma'am.

Then go into the opposite room and wait till I come.

On the stairs we met a burly gentleman with sharp, suspicious eyes. His hands smelled of scented soap. I had no idea then of the part he was to play in my life.

I crossed the landing and opened the door. The room had once been very grand but everything in it was coated in dust and dropping to pieces. Some sort of feast moldered[1] on the table.

1. moldered: crumbled or decayed.

There was a rattling of mice in the skirting[1] and all sorts of crawly things were running about. Suddenly there was a hand on my shoulder.

This is where I shall be laid when I am dead.

What do you think that is?

I can't guess what it is, ma'am.

It's a great cake. A bride-cake. Mine!

Come! Walk me!

My job was to walk her round and round, while she gazed on the moldering feast.

Later, in the overgrown garden, I bumped into a pale young gentleman of my own age.

Who gave you leave[2] to prowl about?

Miss Estella.

Come and fight.

Why is he dancing about like that? Is that how gentlemen fight?

Laws of the game! Regular rules!

I struck the first blow.

FLUMP!

I was never so surprised in my life!

He kept getting up, and I kept knocking him down.

You've won. Shake hands.

Can I help you?

No, thankee.

Soon he was bruised all over. I had to admire his spirit.

You may kiss me if you like.

She offers it like a piece of money.[3] It doesn't mean anything.

1. skirting: baseboard.   2. leave: permission.
3. like a piece of money: She looks down at him, like a rich person giving a coin to a beggar.

My Apprenticeship

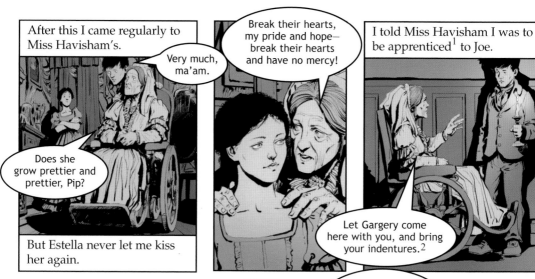

After this I came regularly to Miss Havisham's.

Very much, ma'am.

Does she grow prettier and prettier, Pip?

But Estella never let me kiss her again.

Break their hearts, my pride and hope— break their hearts and have no mercy!

I told Miss Havisham I was to be apprenticed[1] to Joe.

Let Gargery come here with you, and bring your indentures.[2]

Joe looked awkward in his Sunday clothes.

There are five-and-twenty guineas[3] in this bag. That is Pip's reward.

I saw Estella's laughing look and felt ashamed of him.

Am I to come again, Miss Havisham?

No. Gargery is your master now.

Now you see, I am one of them that always go right through with what they've begun.

The villain!

Pumblechook claimed the credit for the 25 guineas!

For one that's bound apprentice, there's no playing cards, or strong liquor, or late hours in bad company—imprisonable offenses, remember, Pip!

Why aren't you enjoying yourself?

My sister lavishly invited friends to a celebratory dinner at the Blue Boar inn.

From now on I worked with Joe, but I felt within me I could never like his trade. I had liked it once, but once was not now.

1. apprenticed: bound by a legal agreement to work for a craftsman for a specified time, to learn his trade.
2. indentures: the contract between a master craftsman and his apprentice.
3. five-and-twenty guineas: A guinea was worth one pound and one shilling; £1.05 in modern money; 25 guineas is £26 and five shillings. This is a generous gift to pay for Pip's apprenticeship.

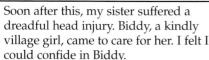

Soon after this, my sister suffered a dreadful head injury. Biddy, a kindly village girl, came to care for her. I felt I could confide in Biddy.

I want to be a gentleman.

Don't you think you're happier as you are?

Biddy, I am disgusted with my calling[1] and my life. I wouldn't mind being so coarse and common, if nobody had told me so!

It was neither a very true nor a very polite thing to say. Who said it?

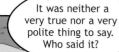

The beautiful young lady at Miss Havisham's. I admire her dreadfully, and I want to be a gentleman on her account.

To spite her or to gain her over[2]?

I don't know.

If it is to spite her, that might be better done by caring nothing for her words.

And if it is to gain her over, I should think she was not worth gaining over.

But still I could not help adoring Estella.

If only I could get myself to fall in love with *you*—you don't mind my speaking so openly to such an old acquaintance?

Oh, dear, not at all! Don't mind me.

If I could only get myself to do it, *that* would be the thing for me.

But you never will, you see.

1. my calling: my trade.
2. gain her over: win her over.

GREAT EXPECTATIONS

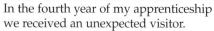

In the fourth year of my apprenticeship we received an unexpected visitor.

Joseph Gargery? You have an apprentice, commonly known as Pip? Is he here?

I am here.

My name is Jaggers, and I am a lawyer from London. I have unusual business with you.

He's the man we met on the stairs at Miss Havisham's!

Now, Joseph Gargery, I am the bearer of an offer[1] to relieve you of your apprentice.

My dream is reality!

You are to understand, Mr. Pip, that the name of your benefactor[4] remains a profound secret until that person chooses to reveal it.

He will come into a handsome property.[2] He is to be brought up as a gentleman — in a word, as a young fellow of Great Expectations.[3]

Miss Havisham is going to make my fortune!

When that may be, I cannot say. You are prohibited from making any inquiry on this head.[5]

You should have some new clothes. Shall I leave you twenty guineas?

I have come into such good fortune, Miss Havisham, and I am so grateful for it.

My heart was beating so fast that I could barely speak.

I was to study in London with Mr. Matthew Pocket. I knew that name—he was a relation of Miss Havisham's!

Be good— deserve it—abide by Mr. Jaggers's instructions.

I said farewell to my fairy godmother. Remembering Jaggers's warning, I did not openly thank her.

1. I am the bearer of an offer: I have come to tell you about an offer made by someone else.
2. a handsome property: a generous amount of money.
3. a young fellow of Great Expectations: a young man who is expected to be very successful in life.
4. your benefactor: the person who is being generous to you.
5. on this head: about this subject.

Goodbye, my dear, dear friend!

Joe wanted to walk me to the coach, but I thought it would spoil my new look.

You're the prowling boy!

And you are the pale young gentleman!

I was to share chambers[1] in London with my tutor's son, Herbert Pocket. I met him on the stairs.

I hope you'll forgive me for having knocked you about so.

That's not quite how I remember it!

I hear you've come into good fortune.

How did you bear your disappointment?

When Miss Havisham was young she fell in love with a man who was only after her money.

I didn't care for her. She's hard and haughty to the last degree.

Miss Havisham sent for me once. Perhaps I should have been engaged to Estella!

Miss Havisham has brought her up to wreak revenge on all the male sex.[2]

The marriage day was fixed, the dresses bought, the guests invited. The day came, but not the bridegroom. He wrote her a letter—

What became of the bridegroom?

He fell into deep shame and ruin.

Which she received when she was dressing? At twenty minutes to nine?

At that hour and minute! She stopped the clocks and has never since looked upon the light of day.

1. chambers: rented rooms.
2. wreak revenge on all the male sex: Estella is being raised to break men's heart for sport.

Mr. Jaggers Entertains

Herbert worked in shipping insurance.

Are the profits large?

Why, n-no: not to me.

That is, it doesn't pay me anything...

I feared he would never be a great businessman.

You'll fall in the river and be drownded,[1] and what'll your pa say then!

The Pockets were not well off. Six small Pockets raced about the garden, but Mrs. Pocket fancied herself too grand a lady to bother what they did.

I'm next heir but one to the baronetcy,[2] you know.

Herbert's father had a second student, called Bentley Drummle. He was sulky, and a worse snob than Mrs. Pocket.

Mr. Jaggers often spoke harshly to me. His clerk, Wemmick, told me not to mind about it.

I hardly know what to make of Mr. Jaggers's manner.

He don't mean you *should* know. He's deep—deep as Australia.

If you'd care to visit me at home, I should consider it an honor.

I should be delighted.

Well, at least he's human.

Thankee. Have you dined with Mr. Jaggers yet?

Not yet.

You'll see a wild beast tamed. It won't lower your opinion of Mr. Jaggers's powers.

When you do—look at his housekeeper.

---

1. drownded: a mispronunciation of "drowned."
2. baronetcy: the rank of baronet (above a knight but below a baron).

Mr. Jaggers's dinner invitation included Herbert and Bentley Drummle.

Bentley Drummle? I like the look of that fellow.

The housekeeper was very pale, with large, faded eyes which she kept fixed on Jaggers.

I could scatter you all like chaff.[1]

Conceited oaf.

The talk turned to rowing. Drummle started boasting of his muscle power.

If you talk of strength, I'll show you a wrist! Molly, let them see your wrist.

Master, please!

There's power here.

I never saw stronger hands, man's or woman's.

I'm glad you like Drummle, sir, but I don't.

No, you keep clear of him. But I like the fellow. I know his sort. If I was a fortune teller—

I never learned what sort of success Mr. Jaggers foresaw for Bentley Drummle.

1. like chaff: like something very light and worthless (chaff is the bits left over from grain after it has been threshed).

Joe's Visit

A letter from Biddy…

Joe coming to visit! What will my friends make of him?

Pip! You have that growed and that swelled and that gentlefolked!

Now that I lived like a fine gentleman, I would gladly have paid to keep him away.

I am glad to see you, Joe.

Not knowing what to do with his hat, he stuck it on the mantelpiece, where it kept falling off.

Thankee, Sir. I'll take whichever is most agreeable to yourself.

Tea or coffee, Mr. Gargery?

The visit was not a success. Joe started calling me "sir." Even Herbert could not put him at his ease. I had not the sense to see that it was my fault.

Joe brought a message from Miss Havisham: Estella was back from abroad and would like to see me.

Biddy, when I asked her to write it to you, she says, "He will be glad to have it by word of mouth. You want to see him—go!"

I have now concluded, Sir, and, Pip, I wish you ever prospering.

Pip, old chap, you and me is not two figures to be together in London.

But you are not going now, Joe?

Think of me in my forge, with my hammer in my hand.

God bless you, dear old Pip, old chap, God bless you.

I was shamed by his simple dignity. I ran after him into the street, but he was gone.

I went to see Miss Havisham next day. At first I did not recognize the elegant lady next to her.

Do you find her much changed, Pip? She was proud and insulting, and you wanted to go away from her.

That was long ago. I knew no better then.

Is *he* changed?

Very much.

Less coarse and common?

Ha!

Estella treated me as a boy still, yet she lured me on.

This is where you gave me my meat[1] and drink.

I don't remember.

Not remember that you made me cry?

You must know that I have no heart—if that has anything to do with my memory.

I fancied I saw some fleeting resemblance in her face—to whom? I looked again and it was gone.

As Estella left to prepare for dinner, Miss Havisham drew my head close to hers.

Love her! I made her what she is that she might be loved. If she tears your heart to pieces, love her!

It sounded like a curse!

I lodged at the Blue Boar, though I knew I should have stayed with Joe.

I love her! I love her! I love her!

Miss Havisham must mean us for each other!

1. meat: food (of any kind).

I Come of Age

When next I visited our town, it was for my sister's funeral. She was laid quietly in the earth, beside our parents' grave.

I am going to try to get the place of mistress[1] at the new school.

How are you going you live, Biddy?

Meanwhile Herbert and I were spending lavishly. On my twenty-first birthday, Jaggers sent for me.

Of course I shall be often down here. I am not going to leave poor Joe alone.

Are you quite sure that you *will* come to see him often?

I was offended by her doubts, though I knew she was right.

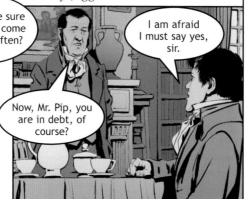

Now, Mr. Pip, you are in debt, of course?

I am afraid I must say yes, sir.

Unfold this piece of paper and tell me what it is.

This is a bank-note for five hundred pounds!

At the rate of that handsome sum per annum[2] you are to live until the donor[3] of the whole appears.

Is my benefactor to be made known to me today?

No. Ask another.

Shall I know soon?

That's a question I must not be asked. That's all I have got to say.

1. mistress: teacher.
2. per annum: each year.
3. donor: giver.

Estella was now in London, being introduced to the fashionable world.

She resents me because she knows Miss Havisham intends me for her. She feels she has no choice.

I saw her at parties, operas, concerts, balls. Her indifference[1] made each event a misery.

It makes me wretched that you encourage a man like Drummle.

He has nothing to recommend him but money.

Don't be foolish, Pip. It's not worth discussing.

Yes it is. I cannot bear that people should say, "She throws away her airs and graces on a boor,[2] the lowest in the crowd."

I can bear it.

She had countless admirers. Bentley Drummle was always hanging about her.

I have seen you give him looks and smiles such as you never give to me.

Do you want me then to deceive and entrap you?

Do you deceive and entrap him, Estella?

Yes, and many others—all of them but you.

1. indifference: complete lack of interest.
2. boor: oaf, lout.

An Unwelcome Visitor

Two years later…

There is someone down there, is there not? What floor do you want?

Mr. Pip.

Alone in our chambers on a wild, windy night, I heard footsteps on the stairs.

It was an elderly man in a rough coat, like a seafarer. To my amazement he held out his arms to me.

You acted noble, my boy. Noble, Pip! And I have never forgot it!

I knew him then, after all those years. It was my convict!

If you have come to thank me for what I did as a child, it was not necessary.

Feeling I had spoken cruelly, I offered him a drink before he went.

May I make so bold as to ask you how you have done so well?

Might a mere warmint[2] ask whose property?

I don't know.

I have been chosen to succeed to[1] some property.

Could I make a guess at your income since you come of age? The first figure now. Five?

Concerning a guardian.[3] Some lawyer, maybe. The first letter of his name, now. Would it be J?

Estella! Estella! Miss Havisham's intentions— all a dream!

The hideous truth came flashing on me. The room seemed to surge and turn.

1. succeed to: inherit.
2. warmint: an undesirable person (a variant of "vermin" or "varmint").
3. guardian: a person who takes the place of a parent for a young person whose parents are dead.

28

So this was my fairy godmother! A criminal, an outcast, guilty perhaps of terrible crimes.

Yes, dear boy, it's me wot has done it!

That dunghill dog wot you kep' life in got his head so high that he could make you a gentleman.

I could not have feared and loathed him more if he had been a wild beast.

I'm your second father, Pip.[1] I've put away money in Australia,[1] only for you to spend. And I've held steady in my mind to come one day and see my boy.

So it was for this wretch and his filthy money that I abandoned Joe!

Mind you, caution is necessary. I was sent for life. It's Death[2] to come back.

How long do you remain?

How long? I'm not a-going back. I've come for good.

Where are you to live? Where will you be safe?

The danger ain't so great. Who knows me here? There's Wemmick and there's Jaggers and there's you. Who else is to inform?

This was all I needed. The man was risking his life for me! I felt I had a duty to protect him.

There is no person who might identify you in the street?

No one bar[3] Compeyson. And no reason to think he's in London.

I found rooms for him nearby and got him some decent clothes—though his past life gave him a savage air no clothes could tame.

I do not know what name to call you. I have given out[4] you are my uncle.

That's it, dear boy, call me uncle. Though my name is Magwitch, christened Abel.

1. Australia: The convict has been transported (sent as punishment) to Australia; see pages 46–47.
2. Death: Under English law, a criminal transported to Australia for life faced the death penalty if he returned.
3. bar: except.
4. given out: announced to many people.

29

MAGWITCH'S TALE

Herbert was the one person I could turn to for advice.

He expects me to live like a lord at his expense. I cannot!

Yet think what he has done for me already!

If you reject him, his desperation might make him give himself up.

That is my dread.

While he is under English law he cannot be safe. We must get him abroad.

He will not leave without me. I must go too.

Once out of England I will tell him gently that we must part.

I needed to know more about Magwitch's past.

In jail and out of jail, in jail and out of jail—that's been my life.

Then I met with Compeyson.

He set up fur[1] a gentleman, this Compeyson. Took me on as pardner[2] and made me his slave.

What was his business?

Swindling, forgery, and suchlike. He'd no more heart than an iron file and was as cold as death.

We were took[3] and tried together, but when evidence was giv', it was always me that seemed to have worked the thing[4] and got the profit.

Compeyson got off lightly for his good character, being known to witnesses in high society—

—and warn't it me was put in irons and sent to Australia?

Herbert passed me a note he had written on the cover of a book.

"Compeyson is the man who professed[5] to be Miss Havisham's lover."

1. He set up fur: He initially looked like.
2. pardner: business partner.
3. took: arrested.
4. worked the thing: committed the crime.
5. professed: pretended.

We had to leave England before Compeyson informed on Magwitch. But first I must see Estella one last time.

Miss Havisham, I am as unhappy as you ever can have meant me to be.

I have found out who my patron[1] is. It was not a fortunate discovery. It seems I came to you only to gratify a whim.[2]

Ay, Pip, you did.

And that Mr. Jaggers—

Mr. Jaggers had nothing to do with it. His being my lawyer is a coincidence.

You made your own snares.[3] I never made them.

But you let me go on in them. Was that kind?

Who am I, for God's sake, that I should be kind?

Estella, you know I love you—that I have loved you long and dearly.

I know love only as a form of words, not in my breast. I have tried to warn you of this.

I see Bentley Drummle always at your side. But you would never marry him?

Better him than a man who would realize I took nothing to him.[4]

Why not tell the truth? I am going to marry him.

It was past midnight when I reached our chambers. The night porter handed me a note in Wemmick's writing.

"DON'T GO HOME."

1. patron: supporter, provider.
2. only to gratify a whim: only because you felt like it.
3. snares: traps. She means that he allowed himself to be taken in by his own imaginings.
4. took nothing to him: had nothing to offer him.

A LIKENESS

Next morning:

Now, Pip, be careful. Don't tell me anything. I don't want to know.

Mr. Jaggers was determined not to get involved.

I drew Wemmick aside to speak more freely.

I heard that your chambers had been watched.

Would it be related to a person called Compeyson?

Wemmick seemed to nod.

I told Mr. Herbert that if he knew of any Tom, Jack, or Richard[1] lodging near you he had better get him out of the way quick.

Mr. Herbert has found a place for him down by the Pool.[2]

Now that's a good spot for three reasons. First: In case of your being followed, it's out of your beat.[3]

Second: Mr. Herbert knows the landlady, so without going near it yourself you can hear of the safety of Tom, Jack, or Richard through him.

Thirdly: If you want to slip Tom, Jack, or Richard on board a foreign packet-boat,[4] there he is—by the river—ready.

After dark I went to the house by the river to tell Magwitch about Wemmick's plan. His manner seemed gentler. I no longer shrank from him.

When the time comes I will go with you.

I've little fear of my safety with such good help, dear boy.

---

1. any Tom, Jack or Richard: someone or other. (The modern phrase is "Tom, Dick, or Harry.")
2. the Pool: the Pool of London—the stretch of the River Thames from London Bridge to Rotherhithe in southeast London. The Pool was the original port of London.
3. out of your beat: Far away from the places you usually go.
4. packet-boat: a boat carrying goods, passengers, and mail on a regular timetable.

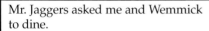

Mr. Jaggers asked me and Wemmick to dine.

So here's to Mrs. Bentley Drummle. You've heard of her marriage, Pip?

Before I could answer, the housekeeper came in. For the first time I saw directly into her face.

Those eyes— I could never mistake them!

And that look, so intent!

Mr. Jaggers was impatient with her. She twitched her fingers nervously, as if she were knitting.

Molly, how slow you are today!

Estella's hands! Estella's face—as years of brutal living would shape it.

That is Estella's mother!

Later I asked Wemmick to tell me more about the housekeeper.

Twenty years ago that woman faced a murder charge— strangling another woman— case of jealousy.

Mr. Jaggers got her off. Managed to argue she hadn't the strength to do it. She has been in his service ever since.

The prosecution claimed she'd killed her child by this man they fought over, to revenge herself on him.

How old was the child—what sex?

Some three years old. Said to have been a girl.

WHAT HAVE I DONE?

Mr. Jaggers had told me Miss Havisham was anxious to see me.

If you can ever bring yourself to say "I forgive her," pray do it.

Perhaps you can never believe now that there is anything human in my heart?

I can do it now. I want forgiveness far too much to be bitter with you.

If you can undo a scrap of what you have done in warping Estella's nature[1]—

Pip, believe me, I meant to save her from misery like mine.[2]

Oh, what have I done? I stole her heart away and put ice in its place.

How did she come to you?

Mr. Jaggers brought her. I had told him I wanted a little girl to rear and love.

What have I done? What have I done?

Might I ask her age then?

Two or three.

She knows only that she was left an orphan and I adopted her.

1. warping Estella's nature: changing her character for the worse.
2. misery like mine: Because Miss Havisham was hurt by the man she loved, she thought she could save Estella by teaching her never to love anyone.

As I was leaving, a coal must have fallen from the fire.

Aaaaah!

My God!

We struggled like desperate enemies—

—I trying to wrap her, she wildly shrieking and trying to free herself.

I dragged the great cloth from the table…

…and the curtains from the windows.

Too late—those eyes that shunned the daylight would never be troubled by it again.

A Bid for Escape

"I sat with Magwitch last night, a good two hours. He improves."

"He spoke of it."

"He is not a bad man. He has had a wretched life."

My hands and arms were badly burned.

"Once there was a woman he was fond of, but she was jealous—vengeful to the last degree."

"They had a child of whom Magwitch was exceedingly fond, but it seems she killed it."

"He could never trace either of them."

"Herbert, I am not feverish, am I? My mind is not wandering?"

"I believe the man we have in hiding down the river is Estella's father."

At last the news came that the coast was clear.

"Burn as soon as read. On Wednesday you might do what you know of. Now burn."

We planned to row Magwitch as far down river as possible before nightfall.

"Beyond Gravesend,[1] the packet-boat is not likely to be searched."

We would stay overnight and hail a foreign vessel next day.

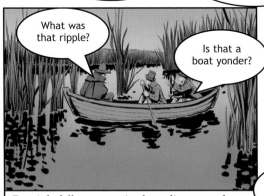

"What was that ripple?"

"Is that a boat yonder?"

By nightfall we were in the solitary reaches of the Thames between Essex and Kent. The fear that we were suspected or followed was always in our minds.

We stopped at a lonely inn.

"They could be Customs men looking for smugglers."

Woken in the night by the creaking inn sign, I saw two men peering into our boat.

36   1. Gravesend: a river port in Kent, on the south bank of the Thames.

There was no sign of them next day as we rowed out to meet the Hamburg[1] steamer.

But suddenly a boat shot out from the bank and drew alongside us.

You have a returned Transport[2] there, name of Abel Magwitch.

I call upon him to surrender, and you to assist.

Stop the paddles!

Compeyson!

The steamer was almost upon us when Magwitch flung himself at one of the passengers in the other boat.

I felt the steamer's impact as the boat sank beneath me. Herbert and I were hauled aboard the police boat.

Magwitch was severely injured.

We went down together and fought under water.

I can't say what I may have done to him, but I broke free.

Compeyson's body was found later.

I knew there was no hope that Magwitch would be spared the death penalty. To think that he had come home for my sake!

Dear boy, I'm quite content to take my chance. I've seen my boy, and he can be a gentleman without me.

How much better a man he is than I have been to Joe.

1. Hamburg: a major port in northern Germany.
2. Transport: a convict who has been transported to Australia.

LOST HOPES AND NEW HOPE

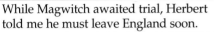

While Magwitch awaited trial, Herbert told me he must leave England soon.

The firm is sending me to Cairo.[1] Would you consider working with me there?

If you thought you could leave the offer open for a while...

For a little while —six months, a year.

Two or three months at most!

By the time of his trial Magwitch was very ill.

God bless you. You've never deserted me, dear boy.

You knew the penalty of returning. You returned. The sentence must be death.

My lord, I have received my sentence of death from the Almighty,[2] but I bow to yours.

I meant to, at first. How little I deserve his faith in me.

I now prayed that he might die before the day of execution.

On my next visit I saw a great change in him. He lay calmly looking at the ceiling.

Dear Magwitch, you had a child whom you loved and lost.

She is living, she is a lady and very beautiful, and I love her.

He smiled.

O Lord, be merciful to him, a sinner.[3]

Then his head dropped quietly onto his breast.

1. Cairo: the capital of Egypt. The English firm that Herbert works for has its own office there.
2. the Almighty: God. Magwitch knows that he is already dying of his illness.
3. O Lord…: Pip is quoting from the Bible, Luke 13:18.

At last I made a decision: I would go back to work in the forge and marry Biddy—if she would forgive my faults. But I was too late!

Dear Biddy, how smart you are! And Joe, how smart *you* are!

It is my wedding day and I am to be married to Joe!

Biddy, you have the best husband in the whole world.

I sold all I had[1] and joined Herbert in Cairo. How could I ever have thought he would not succeed in business? *I* was the one who lacked judgment.

It was eleven years before I could visit Biddy and Joe.

We giv' him the name of Pip for your sake.

You must marry too, Pip, and have a son.

The child seated by the fire was like my younger self.

We spoke of Estella. Her brutal husband was dead.

Are you sure you don't still fret for her, Pip?

That poor dream has all gone by, Biddy.

Miss Havisham's house was gone, but in the garden was a lone figure.

Estella!

I came to take leave of the poor old place before it was built over.

I have often thought of you—very often.

You have always held your place in my heart.

Suffering has taught me how your heart once suffered.

I have been bent and broken—I think, into a better shape.

Be good to me and tell me we are friends.

We are friends.

And will continue friends apart.

As we left that ruined place together, I saw no shadow of another parting.[2]

1. I sold all I had: Pip is no longer rich. When Magwitch was condemned to death, all his money was confiscated by the government.
2. no shadow of another parting: no danger that we would part again.

The End 39

CHARLES DICKENS (1812–1870)

Charles Dickens was easily the most popular novelist writing in English in the 19th century, and many people would agree that he was the greatest.

He was born in 1812 to moderately well-off parents (his father was a naval clerk), but the family's lifestyle changed when his foolishly extravagant father was arrested for debt and sent to the Marshalsea, a notorious debtors' prison. While Charles's mother and the younger children joined his father in the prison, Charles, who was only 12, was sent to live alone in a lodging house in North London. There he worked 12 hours a day in a boot-blacking (shoe polish) factory to earn the family some money. He never forgot this experience. It taught him the conditions in which poor people lived and worked. Later, as a successful novelist, he used his writing to expose such injustices.

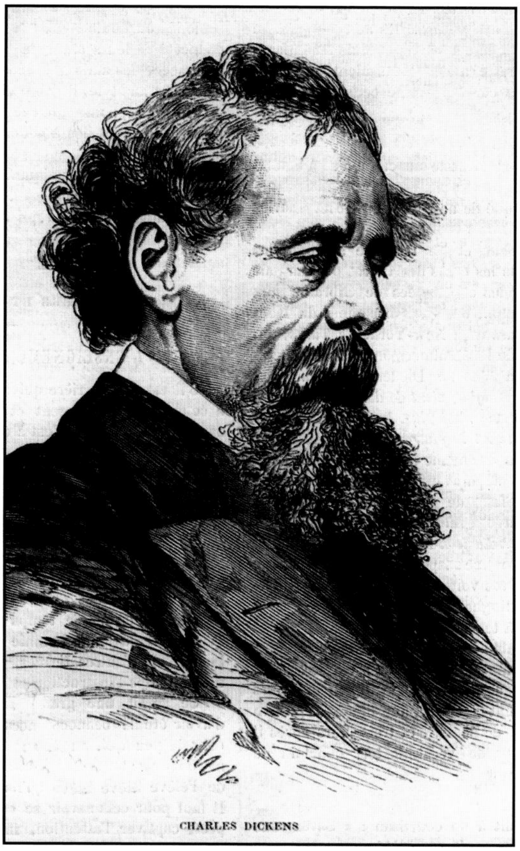
CHARLES DICKENS

An engraved portrait of Charles Dickens

BECOMING A WRITER

The family's fortunes improved enough for Dickens to return briefly to school, but at 15 he had to start work as a clerk in a solicitor's office. He escaped from this boring job by teaching himself shorthand and becoming a parliamentary journalist. He was a quick and lively reporter with a great relish for oddities of character. Soon he was writing humorous articles based on his observations of London life. A collection of these, published in 1836 as *Sketches by Boz,* was such a success that he was immediately invited to write another book. This was *The Pickwick Papers,* which appeared in 1837 and was a runaway success.

SERIALS

From this moment Dickens never looked back. As soon as one book appeared, his readers were impatiently waiting for the next. He was constantly at work, often starting on a new book while he was still writing installments of the previous one. All his major novels first came out as serials in magazines. This meant that people who couldn't afford the price of an expensive three-volume novel could still buy his work. This was important to Dickens, who loved to feel that he was in touch with a wide public and could stir their consciences through his writing.

A BUSY LIFE

Dickens had enormous energy. As well as completing 14 full-length novels and countless shorter pieces, he was also a journalist, magazine editor, lecturer, travel writer, playwright, and amateur actor. He used his acting skill to great effect in giving public readings from his novels, mesmerizing audiences by his ability to conjure up vivid characters. He took these performances on tour in England and the United States. One particularly gruelling series of 76 readings which he gave in America in the winter of 1867–68 finally broke his health, and he died two years later, aged 58. He was at work on his unfinished novel *The Mystery of Edwin Drood* on the day before he died.

DICKENS THE SOCIAL CRITIC

In his novels Dickens was a fierce critic of the poverty and inequality he saw all around him in Victorian society. He campaigned for parliamentary reform, better schooling, better housing and sanitation, and for the abolition of slavery. His greatest asset in getting people to think seriously about these things was his ability to entertain. His novels are all good stories, packed with characters whose quirks and oddities can be sinister, endearing, or hilarious, and who all have that larger-than-life quality that we still call "Dickensian."

BOOKS BY CHARLES DICKENS

1836: *Sketches by Boz*
1837: *The Pickwick Papers*
1838: *Oliver Twist*
1839: *Nicholas Nickleby*
1841: *The Old Curiosity Shop*
1841: *Barnaby Rudge*
1843: *A Christmas Carol*
1844: *Martin Chuzzlewit*
1845: *The Cricket on the Hearth*

1850: *David Copperfield*
1853: *Bleak House*
1854: *Hard Times*
1857: *Little Dorrit*
1859: *A Tale of Two Cities*
1861: *Great Expectations*
1865: *Our Mutual Friend*
1870: *The Mystery of Edwin Drood*
    (unfinished)

GREAT EXPECTATIONS

Great Expectations grew out of a publishing crisis. In the autumn of 1860 Dickens' recently launched weekly magazine, *All the Year Round,* was in trouble. It relied on a good serial to keep readers buying, and the current one, "A Day's Ride" by Irish writer Charles Lever, was a flop. Sales were falling fast. Dickens called "a council of war" at the magazine's office and determined that "the one thing to be done was for me to strike in." He started in October with his usual energy, and by the end of the month four weekly episodes had been "ground off the wheel," as he put it. The first installment of *Great Expectations* came out in December, and within a few weeks it had saved the fortunes of *All the Year Round.*

THE STORY OF A LIFE

The book that began as a rescue operation proved to be one of Dickens' best-loved works and, some think, his finest. Like that other great favorite, *David Copperfield*, it tells the story of a small boy growing up and entering the world, as remembered by himself as an older man. As in *David Copperfield*, too, the hero's most deeply felt experiences are based on events in Dickens' life. Both David and Pip have painful childhoods and feel shame about certain aspects of their lives. This reflects the 12-year-old Dickens' intense misery and sense of betrayal at being sent by his parents to work in a rat-infested blacking factory (a fact which he hid all his life), and the humiliation of knowing that his father was in prison.

But whereas *David Copperfield* tells of disadvantages overcome and effort rewarded with happiness, Pip's is a story of undeserved wealth, unrealistic hopes, and mistaken priorities.

Eleven years separates the writing of the two books and, though the sensational plot of *Great Expectations* owes nothing to Dickens' own life, its darker tone reflects the experiences of his later years. The collapse of his marriage and the divisions in his family had made him very much aware of the hurts that people can inflict on one another. The novel shows this destructive process at work. Pip harms Joe and Biddy through his selfish vanity, Miss Havisham warps Estella through her desire for revenge, and Estella tortures Pip with her lack of humanity.

AN UNHEROIC HERO

Pip is a complex character. There is the older narrator looking back on his youth and judging himself with the sadness of experience, and there is the much younger Pip with all his fears and hurts and longings. The older Pip makes no excuses for his shabby treatment of Joe or his condescending attitude to Herbert Pocket. He is an unheroic hero, certainly no better than the rest of us, but he is not an unlikeable one. Like most people, he wants to be rich, to be loved, and to be happy. At the end of the book Dickens leaves us to decide whether he has achieved all—or any—of these goals.

STAGE AND SCREEN

Stage adaptations of the novel appeared soon after its publication. There were several American versions in the 1860s. In a British version by W. S. Gilbert (later of Gilbert and Sullivan fame) in 1871, Pip was played by an actress.

Later stagings included a highly successful 1939 shoestring production by Alec Guinness (who played Herbert Pocket). It was seen by British film director David Lean and inspired his 1947 film version, still a contender for the best-ever Dickens film version. Lean's film opens with a now-famous sequence of the twilit marshes, with gallows and creaking branches, in which Magwitch makes an appearance of truly heart-jolting suddenness. John Mills, though a little too old for the part, makes an agreeable adult Pip, and Martita Hunt's eerie Miss Havisham has a spectacular death. Lean cheated a little at the end, making Estella—jilted by Drummle when he finds out who her parents are—retreat to Miss Havisham's rooms to relive her role. Pip discovers her there, lets in the daylight, and they rush out into sunlight and happiness. Over fifty years later, in 1989, Jean Simmons, who played the young Estella in Lean's film, became Miss Havisham in a six-part BBC television serial.

In 1998 Alfonso Cuarón filmed an updated transatlantic version with Robert de Niro as Magwitch and Gwyneth Paltrow as Estella. Pip is an orphan in a fishing village on the Florida coast, where he encounters the Miss Havisham character, now with cigarette holder and heavy make-up, and with her wedding banquet laid out on the lawn of her moldering mansion. Pip's artistic talents are launched on the New York art world by a mysterious benefactor, and all ends happily.

Finlay Currie as Magwitch and Tony Wager as young Pip in the 1947 David Lean film version of Great Expectations.

43

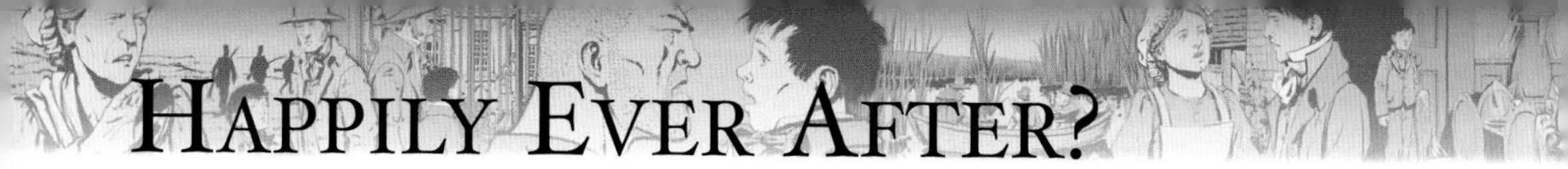

Happily Ever After?

Did Pip marry Estella? Readers have been debating that question ever since *All the Year Round* delivered the last installment. On the face of it, he does. Estella's wretched marriage to Bentley Drummle has taught her the meaning of suffering and the value of love. She tells Pip they will continue friends apart, but he senses a change of heart in her: "I saw no shadow of another parting from her." But Pip has never been good at seeing what the future holds. Is this another of his illusions? Could there be shadows ahead after all?

Two endings

There is another ending—the one that Dickens originally intended. It exists in the form of a proof (a print that the printer sent to the author for checking before publication). In this version, Pip, having heard of the death of Estella's brutal first husband and of her second marriage to a country doctor, meets her by chance as he is walking in London with little Pip (the son of Joe and Biddy). She calls Pip to her carriage and shakes hands with him. "The lady and I looked sadly enough at one another," he recalls. Estella asks to kiss the child, which she assumes is Pip's own, and then they part. Pip reflects that he is glad of the meeting, for her tone and look have shown him "that suffering had been stronger than Miss Havisham's teaching, and had given her a heart to understand what my heart used to be."

In this version Pip's love for Estella is a thing of the past, another unfulfilled expectation which a wiser, more realistic Pip has given up. It brings the book to a somber close and leaves Pip an emotionally unfulfilled figure—"quite an old bachelor," as he describes himself to Biddy.

The novelist Edward Bulwer-Lytton, a friend of Dickens, read the proofs of *Great Expectations* and urged Dickens to change the ending, which he thought was too bleak and might make the novel less popular. Authors usually don't like to be told they have gotten it wrong, but Dickens was an entertainer who didn't want to disappoint his audience. So he took his friend's advice and wrote the present ending, which comforts readers who are romantic, without seeming too unlikely to hard-headed realists.

But many critics believe that Dickens was wrong to make the change, and that a happy ending contradicts the spirit of the book. Readers who feel that Estella belongs to the world of false values, of glitter without heart, would have to agree.

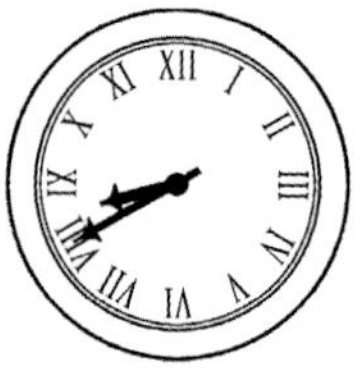

THE LANDSCAPE OF THE NOVEL

From 1817 to 1822 the Dickens family lived at Chatham in Kent in England. These were happy years for Dickens. He went on long walks with his father, who taught him a love of the Kent countryside that stayed with him all his life. A favorite expedition took them past a house called Gad's Hill Place in the village of Higham. It seemed a truly grand building to a small boy, and his father told him that if he worked hard he might someday live in it. Dickens never forgot this. When he was wealthy and famous he bought his childhood dream house. Much of *Great Expectations* was written there.

The countryside around Gad's Hill is the landscape of Pip's childhood. The churchyard of the opening chapter is based on St. Mary's, Higham, Dickens' parish church. Looking from the churchyard wall it was possible in Dickens' day to see, just as Pip did, an old gallows on the marshes that had once held the body of a pirate.

Joe's forge was modelled on the smithy at Chalk, the village where Dickens spent his honeymoon. The forge and the house attached to it were at one time just as described in the book. To this day part of the roof comes to within a yard or so of the ground, which makes sense of Uncle Pumblechook's theory that the convict must have stolen the pie by climbing onto the roof and letting himself down the chimney.

"Our nearest town," where Miss Havisham lived, is modelled on Rochester near Chatham. The original of Miss Havisham's house is Restoration House, a 17th-century brick mansion just off Rochester High Street. It is entered through an iron gate like the one Estella opens for Pip, and across a paved yard, just as in the novel.

Despite knowing Kent so well, Dickens did careful research. In May 1861, while working on the the last chapters of *Great Expectations,* he hired a steamer for the day and took a party of friends down the Thames from Blackwall in London to Southend. For them it was a summer jaunt; for him it was the way to ensure that the details of Magwitch's escape bid matched reality.

Area shown
on main map

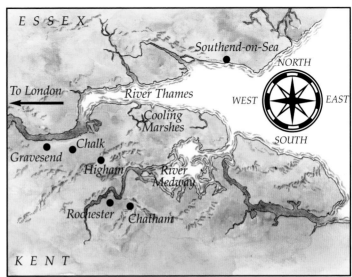

CRIME AND PUNISHMENT

In the making of *Great Expectations*, Dickens the critic of Victorian society seems much less active than Dickens the storyteller. The book does not attack poverty and inequality directly. We see the story through Pip's eyes, and he does not always understand the implications of what he sees and hears.

But Dickens expects *us* to be alert to what Pip sees and hears. He uses Pip's changing relationship with the convict Magwitch to plead for a much more compassionate understanding of the causes of crime. Pip as a child naturally sees the convict as a figure of terror. Only Joe with his simple goodness recognizes the suffering human being in him:

"We don't know what you have done, but we wouldn't have you starved to death for it, poor miserable fellow-creature.—Would us, Pip?"

VICTORIANS AND CRIME

The reappearance of Magwitch as the horrendous nighttime caller at Pip's lodgings is one of the great scenes in the book. In his mind Pip rejects him instantly and utterly—and the reader, who knows the personal tragedy that Magwitch's revelation means for Pip, can probably forgive him for this. But Pip's instinctive loathing is a reflection of prosperous Victorian society's reaction to crime. The Victorians feared and repressed crime without seeking to understand its causes. From this moment Pip and the convict are bound to each other, and Dickens uses every stage in their developing relationship to

show how extreme poverty and social neglect will distort the nature of those who might be capable of good.

A great part of Pip's horror of Magwitch is fear of what he may have been guilty of in the past—the Victorian dread of "innate [inborn] wickedness." Dickens lets Magwitch's life-story speak for itself. An orphan, without a soul to care for him, his earliest memories are of stealing food to stay alive. So it was:

"In jail and out of jail . . . a ragged little creetur as much to be pitied as ever I see . . . 'This is a terrible hardened one,' they says . . . 'May be said to live in jails, this boy.' . . . They always went on agen me about the Devil. But what the Devil was I to do? I must put something into my stomach, mustn't I?"

There is an echo of Pip's childhood here. Like Magwitch, he was orphaned as a baby and abused as a child—but at least Mrs. Joe fed him, however uncaringly, and most importantly he had Joe's unquestioning love. By the end of the book Pip realizes that Magwitch's boundless gratitude for a single act of kindness reveals a nobler spirit than Pip had shown in his dealings with Joe.

TRANSPORTATION

Uneducated and ruffianly, Magwitch commits the same crime as the "gentlemanly" Compeyson but receives double the sentence. Serving their terms in the same prison ship, they escape separately and are retaken while fighting each other. No one believes Magwitch's claim that he was trying to ensure Compeyson's arrest, and he is transported to Australia for attempted murder.

Transportation was an alternative sentence for many crimes that were punishable by death. These even included pick-pocketing and shoplifting, which we now think of as minor crimes. Returning from transportation carried the death penalty until 1834.

The idea of removing undesirable elements in the population by sending them overseas dates from the earliest time that Britain had colonies to send them to. In the 17th century they were shipped to North America. That destination was closed in 1775 when Britain's American colonies declared their independence; Australia became the substitute. In 1778 the Australian colony of New South Wales received its first shipload of 778 convicts, of whom 192 were women. By the time transportation was ended in 1868, Britain had sent 165,000 convicts to Australia.

Transported convicts were set to work on official projects such as road building and mining, or assigned to landowners as unpaid labor. When they had finished their sentence they were free to work for themselves, although they were not free to leave the country. This is how Magwitch came to make himself a fortune breeding sheep.

PRISON HULKS

Through lack of prison space, growing numbers of convicts awaiting transportation were held aboard the disused battleships (hulks) that were rotting on the Thames and Medway rivers. Parliament authorized their use for two years in 1776, but the temporary measure soon became permanent and hulks were used as floating jails for all kinds of offenders, not just those awaiting shipment to Australia. Magwitch and Compeyson were together in one, before Magwitch was sentenced to transportation.

Conditions aboard these floating prisons were dreadful, with little sanitation or proper medical attention. Diseases such as dysentery and "jail fever" spread quickly, and there was an appalling death rate.

Most hulks were decommissioned during the 19th century, though even today prisoners are still sometimes held aboard ships.

The prison hulk Discovery *at Deptford, south London, 1818–1834*

INDEX

IF YOU ENJOYED THIS BOOK, YOU MIGHT LIKE TO TRY THESE OTHER TITLES IN BARRON'S *GRAPHIC CLASSICS* SERIES:

Adventures of Huckleberry Finn Mark Twain

Beowulf Anonymous

David Copperfield Charles Dickens

Dr. Jekyll and Mr. Hyde Robert L. Stevenson

Dracula Bram Stoker

Frankenstein Mary Shelley

Gulliver's Travels Jonathan Swift

Hamlet William Shakespeare

The Hunchback of Notre Dame Victor Hugo

Jane Eyre Charlotte Brontë

Journey to the Center of the Earth Jules Verne

Julius Caesar William Shakespeare

Kidnapped Robert Louis Stevenson

The Last of the Mohicans James Fenimore Cooper

Macbeth William Shakespeare

The Man in the Iron Mask Alexandre Dumas

The Merchant of Venice William Shakespeare

A Midsummer Night's Dream William Shakespeare

Moby Dick Herman Melville

The Odyssey Homer

Oliver Twist Charles Dickens

Robinson Crusoe Daniel Defoe

Romeo and Juliet William Shakespeare

A Tale of Two Cities Charles Dickens

The Three Musketeers Alexandre Dumas

Treasure Island Robert Louis Stevenson

20,000 Leagues Under the Sea Jules Verne

White Fang Jack London

Wuthering Heights Emily Brontë